The Aristocats is based on the book by Thomas Rowe.
Published by Hachette Partworks Ltd.
ISBN: 978-1-909766-80-8
Date of Printing: June 2017
Printed in Romania by Canale

Duchess the white cat lived in Paris with the elegant Madame Bonfamille. Duchess had three kittens – Toulouse, who loved to paint, Marie, who preferred to sing, and Berlioz, who played the piano.

Madame was proud of her talented kittens, but Edgar, her butler, secretly hated looking after them.

One day, Madame called her lawyer George Hautecourt to the house. She wanted to make a will.

"I would like to leave everything to my beloved cats as long as they live," she said. "Then, after they are gone, the rest of my fortune will go to Edgar."

Edgar was listening at the door. He wasn't at all happy to come second to Madame's cats!

"Those cats have got to go," fumed Edgar. Straight away, he dreamt up a wicked plan. That evening, he mixed up sleeping pills with the cats' favourite food. Once the cats were asleep, he would take them somewhere far, far away – and the inheritance would be all his!

The cats shared the tasty treat with Roquefort, their mouse friend.

When all the cats were fast asleep, Edgar bundled them into a basket. Nobody saw him load the basket into his motorcycle sidecar and set off for the countryside. "I'll make sure those cats will never find their way back to Paris," Edgar said to himself.

Suddenly, the motorcycle hit a big bump in the
road. Edgar's hat went flying, and so did the basket
of sleeping cats! The basket landed on a riverbank as
Edgar turned round and sped back towards Paris.

The next morning, when Duchess and the kittens woke up, they got a nasty surprise.

"Where are we?" cried Toulouse.

"Don't be afraid, my darlings," said Duchess, even though she too was very scared.

Just then, Duchess spotted a
cheery, mischievous-looking cat,
strolling on the opposite bank.
"Hello," he called. "I'm
Abraham de Lacy Giuseppe
Casey Thomas O'Malley –
O'Malley the alley cat!"
"My name is Duchess,"
said Duchess shyly.
"Beautiful!" replied O'Malley.
"And your eyes… they're just
like sapphires!"

"Can you show us the way back to Paris?" Duchess asked. "I'll do better than that – I'll take you there!" replied O'Malley.

Just then, a milk van came trundling along the road. O'Malley leapt onto the bonnet, causing the driver to slam on the brakes.

"All aboard!" said O'Malley, guiding his new friends into the back of the van. Soon, they were all tucking into a delicious breakfast of fresh cream. But when the angry milkman spotted them in his mirror, they had to leap off the van in a hurry!

Luckily, they soon found the road to Paris.

The cats followed some railway tracks onto a
bridge over a river. "Let's play trains!" said Toulouse.
"Whoo-whoo!" But then they heard the whistle of a
real train – and it was heading straight for them! In
the nick of time, the cats took cover under the tracks.

Then poor Marie fell into the river!
"Mama!" mewed the terrified kitten.
"Keep your head up,
Marie! Here I come!"
yelled O'Malley, diving
into the icy water.

O'Malley dragged
Marie to safety.
"Thank you
Thomas," gasped
Duchess. "You
saved my little
girl's life!"

Meanwhile in Paris, the newspapers were full of the story of the cats' disappearance.

Roquefort was on the hunt for clues when he overheard Edgar talking to his horse, Frou-Frou. He seemed nervous. "If the police find my hat, they'll know that I'm the cat-napper!" he said.

Now Roquefort knew the truth. But where could his friends be?

Later, at nightfall, the cats finally reached Paris.
"I know a shortcut," said O'Malley, leading the
others over the city rooftops. Duchess and the
kittens had never seen such a wonderful view.
"Wow, this is great!" exclaimed Toulouse.

The sound of a trumpet
floated up from below.
"Is that music?" asked
Berlioz. "It's jazz," explained
O'Malley.
Scat-Cat, an old friend
of O'Malley's, was tooting
a trumpet with his band of
musical jazz-cats. "Come on,
we'll stay here for the night."

In no time, Scat-Cat and O'Malley were singing a duet and everyone was dancing.

"It's not Beethoven, but it sure bounces!" giggled Berlioz.

"Let's swing it, Thomas!" said Duchess as the pair began to dance. Everyone had a wonderful time.

After the party was over, Duchess told O'Malley that she would have to go home the next day.

"Madame will be so worried about us," she explained.

So the next morning, O'Malley took Duchess and the kittens home. When Edgar opened the door, the kittens all raced inside.

Angrily, Edgar threw all the cats into a sack, took
it out to the stables and put it into a trunk.

"You're going to Timbuktu and you're never coming
back!" he snarled. Any minute, the post van would
arrive to collect the trunk and take it to Africa!

Luckily, Roquefort had seen everything. The brave little mouse ran to fetch help. He found O'Malley, who told him to round up Scat-Cat and the rest of the gang. Edgar was in for a very nasty surprise!

While Scat-Cat and his friends kept Edgar busy, Roquefort and O'Malley rescued Duchess and her kittens. And somehow in all the commotion, evil Edgar ended up in the trunk instead!

Madame was overjoyed to have Duchess and the kittens home. When she saw O'Malley, she exclaimed, "What a handsome young man! Shall we keep him in the family?" Duchess was thrilled!

As for Edgar, the post van arrived and he ended
up in Timbuktu, where he could do no more harm.

The kittens were delighted with their new father.
Now O'Malley was no longer an alley cat – he had
joined high society!